DETROIT PUBLIC LIBRARY

3 5674 01837446 3

DETROIT PUBLIC LIBRARY

CHILDREN'S LIBRARY
5201 Woodward
Detroit, MI 48202

DATE DUE STACKS

DATE DUE

W9-CMU-464

For my family

I Want Mama

by Marjorie Weinman Sharmat

Pictures by Emily Arnold McCully

19

84 14144

A

Harper & Row, Publishers
New York, Evanston, San Francisco, London

JE
c. 3

I WANT MAMA

Text copyright © 1974 by Marjorie Weinman Sharmat
Illustrations copyright © 1974 by Emily Arnold McCully
Printed in the U.S.A. All rights reserved.
Library of Congress Catalog Card Number: 74–3584
Trade Standard Book Number: 06–025563–6
Harpercrest Standard Book Number: 06–025554–4
FIRST EDITION

CL

JUN '75

CL

Mama's in the hospital.
She went there to have an operation.
Daddy carried her suitcase and her coat.
I said, "Don't go, Mama."
Mama said, "I'll be back soon."

I felt funny when Mama left.
I drank some milk.

I took a walk in the sun.

I looked up the word "operation" in the dictionary.

Today's Tuesday. I want Mama home.
I want her home *now*.
Mama's chair is empty

and her side of the bed is empty,
and the scrapbook we're making together
is stopped at an empty page.

I can't visit Mama. I'm not old enough
to visit in the hospital.

But I write her cards
and take them to the mailbox
and drop them inside
and then make sure they go down.

My best friend is Sarah,
and her mother has never been in the hospital
except to have babies. Yesterday, I said to Sarah,
"How come your mother has never been sick
in the hospital?"
Sarah didn't answer.
I don't want Sarah's mother to be sick.
I want my mother to be well.

Mama shouldn't have said she'd be home soon.
Soon has been over with for a long time.
I think Mama's never coming back.
She's never going to brush back my hair again
or find where I put my green socks
when I've given up looking.
I don't care about my hair or my socks. Just Mama.
I want to show Mama the new magic trick I learned.
But I don't care about the magic trick. Just Mama.

Yesterday I woke up and said,
"Mama's coming home today!
I know it. I know it. I know it."
But it wasn't so.

I called Mama up. Her voice sounded slow.
"Does anything hurt, Mama? Are you sitting up
when you talk to me?"

Mama said nothing hurt.
She said my voice sounded good.
"I'll make you some presents, Mama.
You'll have the record of having the most presents
that anybody ever had in that hospital."

After I hung up,
I made presents from scrap paper and cloth.
Daddy took them to the hospital after the paste dried.

If I could go to the hospital,
I could find out everything for myself.
I could sneak up the back stairs,
and put on a doctor's uniform, and get into Mama's room
by carrying a glass of water or a thermometer
or a pill or something.
But I would be the smallest doctor in that hospital,
and I would get caught and that would make more trouble
for Mama.

Maybe if I promise to tell the whole truth
for the rest of my life, Mama will come back. Maybe she won't.
What if all of a sudden *I* got sick.
I could go to the hospital and get in bed beside Mama.

But then Daddy would be alone.

Daddy's coming home from visiting Mama.
I see him walking up the steps.
He's smiling. A real smile.

Daddy opens the door. He hugs me.
"Mama's coming home in three days!" he shouts.
I shout too. "Three days! Three!"
Then I ask, "Will Mama be different when she comes back?"
"Mama will be Mama. The same as always," Daddy says.

I run around the house shouting, "Three, three, three!"
It's now my favorite number.
Tomorrow my favorite number will be two.

I'm going to draw a Welcome Home sign and pictures for every room in the house.

I'm going to clean up the whole house,
including the parts that don't show.

I'm going to tell Sarah
that nobody's mother
will be in the hospital.

Mama, Mama, Mama!
Mama's coming home!